A SLIVER OF GLASS

and
Other Uncommon Tales

A SLIVER
OF GLASS

and
Other Uncommon Tales

—— Anne Mazer ——

Hyperion Books for Children
New York

Printed in United States of America.

First Edition
1 3 5 7 9 10 8 6 4 2

This book is set in 13-point Weiss.
Designed by Lara S. Demberg.

Library of Congress Cataloging-in-Publication Data
Mazer, Anne.
A sliver of glass and other uncommon tales / Anne Mazer. — 1st
ed.
p.   cm.
Contents: Glass heart — Hello darling — Sleeping beau — Secrets
— The golden touch — Call me sometime — Stuck — Thin — The
perfect bed — Through the mirror — Swan sister.
ISBN 0-7868-0197-2 (trade)—ISBN 0-7868-2165-5 (lib. bdg.)
1. Children's stories, American. 2. Horror tales, American.
[1. Short stories. 2. Horror stories.] I. Title.
PZ7.M47396S1   1996
[Fic]—dc20   95-45992

For Marcia Menter—

"Meet me at the old bell church . . ."

CONTENTS

1

GLASS HEART

Listen. This is a true story. When I was ten years old a mirror shattered and a sliver of glass flew in my eye. The doctors removed it, but a fragment remained, no bigger than a grain of sand.

At first I felt it as a point of cold that spread from my eye across my face, down my neck, and into my chest. For a while it seemed as though ice water flowed in my veins, and I couldn't get warm no matter how many sweaters, blankets, or furs I piled on top of myself. My family laughed. . . . They didn't understand how piercing a cold that little sliver created in me.

All day long I begged for warmth. The more layers that were piled on me, the more the icy shocks penetrated to the marrow of my bones, till I could hardly bear it and cried out to be cast whole into a fire.

But even if I had thrown myself on a pyre, the cold in me would have only burned more fiercely. The sun brought on chills, as did fires and stoves and the heat of another person. If my mother tried to hold me in her arms, I shivered uncontrollably and jerked away from her.

I cried at night, my hands and feet were so cold. My mother heated bricks in the fireplace and put them in my bed, but nothing could warm me; not the blankets and furs, not the hottest August day, not boiling tea—which seemed to turn to ice as soon as it touched my tongue.

Only when I put my hand into the icy current of the ocean did my shaking and trembling subside. There, like met like. I plunged into the frigid water and stayed until it turned dark and my brother pulled me ashore.

*   *   *

When the first frosts came, I no longer begged for blankets, furs, and fires. The coldness that had penetrated to my marrow, that had seeped into my hands, my blood, my bones, seemed to harden and solidify. Ice formed in my veins. . . . I could imagine myself skating up and down them like they were rivers frozen solid in the dark winter afternoons. I pricked my finger once and watched the blood drip slowly onto the floor, where it congealed in little frozen puddles.

"She has ice water in her veins," my family said.

My eyes faded to pale blue and my hair turned white. My skin became cold and marblelike. I lost the sense of smell and touch and color, as though every texture had been bleached out of me. The sensation of cold permeated everything. My hearing—and my thoughts—were clear and sharpened. The shrill voices of insects rang in my ears. I heard footsteps crunching over snow from miles away.

I wore thin shirts in driving winds, went barefoot over frozen fields, and slept outside under boughs laden with heavy white snow. Boys and girls threw stones at me, but the ones that hit me never left a mark. I barely felt them. Nothing could touch me anymore.

*   *   *

Imagine yourself slowly freezing. First the eyes, then the hands, the blood, the muscles, and bone. The coldness, the color leaking out of eyes and heart.

That sliver of glass, which radiated intense cold like a sun, pierced my heart one day. Then I could hear and see even more clearly than before, and my mind became like a knife.

2

HELLO, DARLING

"Hello, darling, it's me."

I looked up from my book and saw a tall girl dressed in jeans, sneakers, and a ripped T-shirt. A big gray cap was pulled down over her face—all I could see was a firm chin and a bit of straight red hair.

She pulled out a chair. "Haven't seen you in ages, have I? So, tell me, what's new? Anything happening?"

"Not much," I said, wondering who she was and where I had met her. At school? The mall? Baseball practice? Or had I seen her in this library last week?

"Well!" she exclaimed. "I wish I could say the same."

Her friendly voice was irresistible. "You've been busy?"

"All day and all night. Not a moment's rest. It's work,

work, work all the time. I can't catch my breath, darling."

I shut my book and sat up in my chair. "Isn't there a law against that?"

"Well, there may be laws, but who pays any attention to them?"

She pushed back the gray cap. She had large blue eyes and a snub nose. Now that I could see her face clearly, she didn't look any more familiar than before.

"Do you go to school?" I asked.

"Do I ever!"

"Whose class?"

"Miss Kink, Mr. Bonk, Mrs. Blink, Ms. Funk . . ."

"Kink, Bonk, Blink, and Funk? Never heard of them!"

She rubbed her cheek with the back of her hand. "You ought to be glad you haven't. The worst teachers in the school. They pile on the work—and no excuses allowed. You have to do it every day—or else. And then, when I get home—more, more, more!"

"Oh no," I said. "Shouldn't you report that to the school guidance counselor?"

"Look at my hands!" She held them in front of my face. They were large, capable-looking hands marked with stars, triangles, half-moons. On her left thumb was a lizard drawn in green ink.

"What's that?"

"My homework assignments for just one night! And I haven't even shown you my feet!"

She kicked off her sneakers. Her big toe had a winged snake winding around it. Her other toes were marked with suns and heads of queens, which nodded slowly as I stared at them.

Little tongues of fire licked at her heels.

"*This* is why I'm up all night," she announced. "Now do you understand, darling?"

"What kind of assignments are these?" I asked.

"Bonk says they're elementary. Funk says they're primary. Blink doesn't say much—she just piles on the work. Kink is a kidder and cracks a joke when I tell her I haven't slept for eighteen days."

"No one can go without sleep for eighteen days!"

"It's tough," she agreed. "Especially when we're not allowed to go home until we finish our assignment."

"You're not allowed to go home?"

"Rules, darling. You know them as well as I."

"I've never heard of them."

"Well, you will. Everyone does, sooner or later."

I cleared my throat. "You go to *this* school?"

"Of course, darling. You see me all the time—don't you?"

"Well, actually . . . no."

Her eyes lit up. "Perhaps I conjured you?"

"I don't think so."

"Ensorcelled you?"

I shook my head.

"Wished you? Dreamt you? Redeemed you?"

"Uh-uh."

"Well, then I must have found you," she said, wiping her hands on her jeans. "There's no other explanation possible."

"I'm not lost," I said.

"Have you ever been?" she asked.

"No!" I said.

"You've never been found?"

"You don't just find people—unless you know them already. These things don't happen here."

She looked thoughtful. "They don't, do they?"

"No."

"Never ever?"

"Absolutely not."

She pushed back a strand of lank red hair. Then suddenly she flung out her arms and began to dance.

"I've done it! I've done it!" she cried. "Hooray for me! Just wait till I tell Blink, Funk, Bonk, and Kink! No more homework! I've finally done it!"

"What have you done?" I asked.

"Why, I've created your world," she answered.

I laughed loudly. "Created my world? That's ridiculous."

"Don't be silly, darling. It's done all the time."

She closed her eyes. Another set of eyes were drawn on the lids, and the pupils moved from right to left, from left to right.

"Open your eyes!" I said.

She opened them. There were small spinning globes inside her eye sockets.

She blinked and they disappeared.

I stared at her, speechless.

"This is what I've been working on in class all year.

You were my homework assignment. You wouldn't believe how hard it was, darling. But now I can graduate!"

She twirled around the room again. "I'm deliriously happy. I've *finally* done it."

"So," I said, trying to understand, "you're saying you created me . . . and my teachers?"

"Of course. Since preschool."

"I don't believe you."

"Remember Miss Adams, Mrs. Stanton, Mrs. Fulmer, Mr. May . . . "

"Anyone could find out their names," I protested.

"What about your parents?" she said. "Your father is an architect who likes ice-cream bars for breakfast. Your mother works in a bank and has a twitch at the corner of her mouth when she gets angry. And you have a sister, too. I thought of everything. She carries mice on her shoulder when your mother isn't around. Wasn't that a clever touch? It's these little details that earn the best grades."

"Our house. You didn't create our house."

"Oh yes, I did," she said. "From the blue velvet couch to the dust under the refrigerator. And the china dishes and the bunk beds and the blackberry bushes in the backyard."

"What about the shopping mall, the movie theater? What about the library? The highway? The bowling alley? The banks, the factory, the airport?"

"I created them all. Didn't I do a good job? I'll probably graduate with honors."

"My books, my friends, my games!" I was yelling now. "My stories! The pictures I draw! My dreams!"

"All mine, darling. All mine."

I wanted to reason with her, tell her how wrong she was. I wanted to name every person I had ever met. But somehow the names, even my own name, would not come to my lips.

"I don't believe you," I said again. I was trembling with anger and fear. "It can't be!"

"Darling, I really have to go now. It's been so good having this chat with you . . . Perhaps we'll do it again soon."

I jumped up. My hands and feet began to tingle. I looked down at them. Was it my imagination, or were they fading at the edges?

She picked up her sneakers and slung them over her shoulder, then yanked the gray cap over her face.

"Wait!" I shouted.

"Good-bye, darling!"

3

SLEEPING BEAU

He woke up late in the night and heard the muffled laughter from the other room. Silverware clattered, plates clinked. Then the shuffling sound of leather slippers on the floor.

"Will we wake the boy?" he heard someone ask.

The man laughed harshly. "He doesn't wake up. Ever!"

The light that crept through the door made patterns on the ceiling of his room. Through his closed eyelids, which were like a transparent skin, he saw everything. He heard the creak of the closet door opening downstairs. Then the door slammed and cars pulled out of the driveway.

They came up the stairs. He knew their heavy tread, the groan of the wood as it gave under their weight.

The door opened.

His breathing came slow and deep, in long, even waves. His eyes were closed. Beneath the sheet, his body lay still, motionless.

For a moment they were silent.

"How sweet and innocent he is," the man whispered.

"A perfect angel," she murmured. "I wish . . ."

She was wearing cologne. It smelled like lilacs, like the breezes that came into his room on spring nights.

"He's safe here, isn't he?" she asked.

"Don't worry," said the man, a little impatiently. Then he added, "It might change."

She sighed.

"Come," he said. "It's late now."

They tiptoed out of the room, shutting the door behind them. The boy drifted into unconsciousness again . . .

*   *   *

How long he had slept in this bed, this room—how many days, weeks, months, years—he didn't know. At first he hadn't realized that he was sleeping. There was only a peace, a darkness, a comfort, as though he were being rocked in a vast ocean.

*   *   *

Then there came moments of light that pierced him and hurt his head. He screamed from the pain, and the woman came running. "What is it?" she said over and over again.

She said to the man, "He's having nightmares."

They stood over him, watching him. Sometimes they

11

touched him. His body felt like wood. He wondered if they were really squirrels that were scampering over his branches.

He fell into a deep sleep again.

*　　　*　　　*

The woman came in sometimes during the day. He saw her in her violet dress, sitting on the polished wooden chair, twisting her wedding ring around and around. She was never able to sit for very long. After a moment she rose and adjusted a picture over his bureau. Then she stood by his bed, staring down at him with a frown on her face.

*　　　*　　　*

One day the pain was gone. And the smell of rotting leaves, of mud and flowers came through an open window.

He breathed it deeply and felt it carrying strength into his body.

The wind bore faraway voices into the room. It was as though the air was singing to him.

Something brushed lightly against his face—a petal, or a curtain, or the wing of a bird.

His eyes flickered open, shut, then open again.

*　　　*　　　*

Long ago, in another life it seemed—when he slept and played and ran like others—he had awoken in the middle of the night and crept down the long, silent hall to his mother and father's room.

He was frightened of the dark. There were shadows

everywhere—behind the clock, under the chairs. And the floor creaked; some machinery far away hummed. Even his breathing sounded very loud and almost strangled.

Their door was closed. He knocked against it with his hand. No one answered.

He knocked again. Still no answer. He imagined them lying on their bed lifeless, like two dolls. Or had they disappeared, slipped out of the house when they thought he was sleeping?

He banged frantically on the door. Suddenly it flew open. His father loomed over him.

"What do you want?"

He couldn't speak.

His father took him by the elbow. Behind him, his mother half rose from the bed.

"What is it?" Her voice sounded low and hoarse, as if she were someone else.

"Go back to your room," his father commanded.

Down the long, dark corridor he ran without stopping until he reached his door. He flew into his room and dove into the bed.

His father's footsteps sounded heavily down the hallway.

The door was slammed shut. The boy heard the sound of a key in the lock.

And then came his father's parting words: "Once we put you to bed, you stay there."

4

SECRETS

Secrets go through the room like the wind over a field of dry grass. Girls whisper in the ears of other girls, the boys huddle together. Their words make trails between the wooden desks, then fly out the window, and past the school, making their way into the world.

There are secrets everywhere—behind cupboard doors, in shadows of coats, in pull-out maps that hang over blackboards. Secrets between pages, where pencil meets paper, in the chalk dust that falls to the floor.

*   *   *

Only the girl with the long brown braids has no secrets to tell.

The other children do not believe her when she tells them she has no secrets. They tease her, plead with her, mock her.

"Impossible," they say. "Everyone has secrets."

"Tell us," they say. "We have to know."

"Little no-secret," they laugh.

When she shakes her head so insistently that the long brown braids fly around her head, they get angry. They push her, they take her pencils, they steal her lunch.

But still she will not tell them any secrets.

Then they become afraid of her and shun her.

*　　*　　*

The girl with the long brown braids is studying a piece of paper on the desk in front of her. It is an ordinary ruled sheet with some writing on it, and it seems as though she is studying for a test or trying to memorize a problem. One of her braids is wrapped around her hand, and from time to time she uncoils it and strikes the paper with it, as though it were a whip.

Occasionally, a girl or boy glances uneasily in her direction, wondering if the words on her paper are secrets. They want her to tell them, but she won't. And why is she hitting the paper with her braid? Over and over she strikes the words as if she would banish them from the paper. Are the words that powerful—or is she thinking of something else altogether? Another, unwritten secret?

She says she has no secrets, but everything she does is a secret. That's what the children think; that's what they know.

Then, once more, they turn their backs on her. They lean forward and begin to whisper. "Did you hear? . . ."

"They said it happened at his house last night . . ."

". . . she ran away . . ."

"His brother . . ."

"Tell me again . . ."

Words drift across the room to the girl with the long brown braids: "snakes," "box," "mother." She feels the words bumping up against her, and she shrugs as if to shake them off. Then she looks at her paper and erases several words, writing over them carefully with a sharp black pencil.

Now the secrets seem to avoid her, to fly around her. She sees herself as an empty space at the center, a hollow, a dome of silence that secrets dare not cross.

*   *   *

When she was four or five years old, she sat on a blanket in the middle of a field. Adults were huddled in little groups, whispering, while the children ran wild. They screamed and climbed trees, rained apples on one another's heads, jumped over ditches, snatched flowers in their fists. When they were tired they dropped to the ground, where they clustered together, telling secrets.

She sat alone on the blanket with a book of pictures open on her lap. She could feel the secrets around her in the air, the humming words making their way from group to group. *Come, come, come,* the secrets said. *Tell us . . .*

The children whispered and beckoned to her. She surely must have a secret. Something simple or amusing or even silly. There were secrets in everyone, even in babies.

Why didn't she run over to them? Why did she sit on the blanket and blindly turn the pages of her book?

The other children kept calling to her, and she did not move. She felt empty, like clear glass, or like air expanding. She was watching the secrets move, leaving long silvery trails that took on different hues as they went from one child to another.

She didn't want their secrets. They would wind their way into her, twist around her thoughts, bind her movements. She wanted to keep herself cool and free and empty.

The children got up to play again, trailing their secrets behind them. Sitting on her blanket, she watched them until the sky darkened and their parents called them to leave.

*   *   *

The girl with the long brown braids is ten now. Her braids are gone. She wears blue jeans and a baseball cap to school and carries a red backpack, which she swings from one arm. The other children stay away from her; no one wants to be her friend. If she were poor and meek, they would feel sorry for her, whisper pitying stories, take her to lunch and feed her sweets from their bags—but she is not poor or meek. So they won't sit with her at the lunch table. They won't share their books with her. They won't do sums on the blackboard when she is there.

She wishes that someone would talk to her. She wants to tell them that they have nothing to fear from her.

She doesn't want to hurt them. It's only that she can see their world of secrets—can see them growing up like weeds, bursting through walls, tangling on the floors, hanging from ceilings—secrets that will eventually choke off all air and make it impossible to move.

She only wants to hack through this thick under-growth with a sword, to clear it out and open it up.

That is her secret.

5

THE GOLDEN TOUCH

For years, M. had thought of nothing but gold. Gold was power; gold was riches; gold was shining, beautiful metal.

Gold filled two of his storehouses. His horses had harnesses of gold; the banisters and washing bowls in his house were made of beaten gold.

His gems and treasures were a means to buy more gold; his wife was someone to adorn in gold. He loved her most when she wore a gold tiara in her hair, a finely woven golden gown, and gold chains around her neck, arms, and ankles. Her hair, too, was long and golden, but how many times had he told her that she would be even more beautiful if it were made of golden wire?

His children received gold coins on their birthdays. M. brought them up to love and revere gold, to hold it above all else.

*   *   *

One day, as M. walked toward the stables to see his favorite horse, something shining caught his eye. Golden dust glittered on the ground beneath his feet. Dropping to his hands and knees, he began scooping it up. More and more gold appeared. He heaped it in mounds like piles of sand. When he reached for a shovel to work more quickly, it turned to gold at his touch.

M. danced around the yard for joy, leaving a trail of golden footprints. Entering the stable, he brushed against a battered wooden trough and a lamp that hung from a hook on the wall. These ordinary objects were now priceless treasures.

A mouse scurried past him, flicking its tail against the edge of his foot. Now it was a golden mouse, a toy, an ornament. M. picked up the little creature and touched it with his lips.

Soon he would have more gold than anyone else on earth.

*   *   *

When he went to his favorite horse, one affectionate pat turned the animal to shining gold. M. tried to feed the remaining horses without touching them, but in his hand the hay changed to golden wire. "The horses will starve," M. said. "Perhaps it is kinder to turn them to gold. And after all, they are still beautiful."

One after another, he stroked the manes of the

remaining horses. His footsteps rang against the golden planks of the floor.

As he left the stable he saw his son carelessly tossing coins in the air. M. hated waste. "Stupid boy!" he shouted.

M. broke off a switch to strike his son, but the stick instantly turned to gold.

When the boy saw this, he backed away from his father.

"Come here!" M. ordered, but his son grabbed his coat and ran away.

"What a treasure," M. said softly, forgetting his anger toward his son; forgetting he even had a son. He caressed the stick gently. Each twig and bud was solid gold.

*   *   *

Clutching the stick, he hurried to the house to show his wife. He didn't see his infant daughter crawling over and reaching up to him. He didn't feel her hand touch his leg, but when his wife screamed, he looked down and saw a small golden statue. Groaning, he embraced his wife. She too turned to gold.

"Better gold than salt," M. said to himself. He threw himself down on the couch, bruising his head on the golden pillow. When he awoke from his nap, he was hungry and thirsty. But there was no one to fetch him a cup of tea, no one to bring him his supper. And when he did his accounts, no small daughter to accompany him from treasure house to treasure house. Only two statues stood by the front door. A small golden child held out her arms to be picked up; a golden woman cried out in horror.

*   *   *

In the library the desk was gold, books stiffened under his hand, and the flames in the fireplace turned to pale gold filament.

By this time his house was entirely gold, even the stairs and the pictures on the walls. His chairs were of gold and so were the rugs. When at last he went to lie down, instead of a soft, welcoming bed, he met cold, shining metal. His shoes turned into gold, but he managed to slip out of them. It was impossible to remove his heavy golden clothes. They rubbed against his arms, leaving raw, red marks on his skin. Nor could he light the lamp; and when he wept, gold dripped off his face in shining globules.

*   *   *

In the morning M. had nothing to eat or drink. Food turned to gold in his mouth. Water froze on his lips. He went to the cornfield, but at a single touch, the stalks rustled and stiffened into beaten gold. The sun blazed down, and the reflection from the cornstalks blinded him. He stumbled to the orchard. He could no longer run, for his clothes held him closely in a rigid embrace. Solid blades of grass stabbed his bare feet as he walked, and he tripped over heavy golden flowers. When he reached for a pear hanging from a branch above his head, it turned hard and heavy. The pear tree now bore golden fruit.

*   *   *

Nothing moved in the yard. The stable was silent. The horses no longer whinnied in their stalls; he could no longer feel their warm breath on his face. M. cried out for his wife and daughter.

"I would do anything to lose this accursed touch!" he cried.

*   *   *

The sun beat on his face, and he slumped down in a stupor. A fly landed on his leg. Dazed, he brushed it away.

The fly hovered around him and then landed again on his arm. "Go away," M. muttered.

Suddenly he sat up. The fly grazed his fingers and flew away.

"Can it be true?" M. made his way to a small stream at the edge of his property. There he scooped water into his hands, then let it flow through his fingers back into the stream—clear, wet, and not at all golden.

M. fell to his knees and thrust his head into the water. He drank until his thirst was quenched.

*   *   *

He walked to town to buy food, noticing with relief that the earth under his feet was brown and dusty. The trees he touched remained green, and when he stopped to rest against a fence, it was still wooden when he set off again.

When he reached the town, people ran from him. M. scattered golden coins over the ground. "Gold!" he cried hoarsely. "As much as you want for a loaf of bread!"

But the townspeople bolted their doors and refused to talk to him.

He pulled out golden pears from his pockets, then flowers, sticks, and bees. "A fortune! A fortune for anyone who gives me a piece of bread."

"You have enough gold!" a women cried. "Go away. You can't have me, too."

Every day of his life, he had eaten fruit from his orchards, and grain from his fields, drunk wine from his vineyards. He had never been hungry. Now he craved food above all else.

M. caught a glimpse of his son, who was watching him from behind a tree. "My son! Help me, my son!" he called.

The boy turned away.

"It's me, your father! Come here! Help me!"

His son began to run.

M. tried to chase after him, but in his grief he stumbled and fell. "My son!" he cried in despair.

The boy did not answer. In a moment he had vaulted over a fence and disappeared from sight.

M. packed up his treasures and walked on, going from one town to the next. The news of his gift had spread. No one knew he had lost it. Men, women, and children fled at the sight of him. At times someone left him a loaf of bread, a few oranges, a jug of water. But no one would speak to him, no one would invite him in, no one would touch him.

As he went from place to place, M. often thought he saw his son. He saw him at the back of a fleeing crowd, he saw him slipping out of a doorway, eating at a market stall, or carrying bags for a few pennies. But whenever he called out the boy vanished. Perhaps it was not even his son.

He began to see the boy everywhere. Every stranger had his face. M. searched the crowds, the alleyways, the parks of each town he passed through. A new kind of hunger had awakened in him.

6

CALL ME SOMETIME

I.

In the beginning, when they called, they didn't say anything.

I would pick up the phone and hear a low-pitched vibration on the other end.

"Sometimes the wires are wacky," my mother said.

I noticed that the calls came in at the same time every day. 8:02 in the morning. 1:15 in the afternoon. 6:57 in the evening. And I was the only one who got them.

If my mother answered, it was one of her friends.

If my father answered, it was a business call.

If my brother answered, someone needed to know the homework assignment.

But when I picked up the phone, the wires hummed.

"Hello?" I said. "Hello? Is anyone there?"

Hhmmmmmmmmmm . . .

"Who is this? What's going on?"

Hhhmmmmmmmmm . . .

"Your girlfriend, Jeremy," my brother teased. He had a girlfriend and thought I should, too.

"Damned nuisance!" my father muttered.

"Are you sure you're not dreaming, Jeremy?" my mother asked.

"Someone's trying to reach him," said my father.

"But who?" I asked.

*   *   *

The phone company came out and checked the phone, the wires, and the cables.

There was nothing wrong with our equipment or hookup.

"They'll get sick of calling sooner or later," my father said.

The calls kept coming in.

"Hello? Hello? Is anyone there?"

Hmmmmmmmmmmmmm . . .

*   *   *

At school I tried to find out if I had a secret enemy.

I asked if any of the other kids had ever gotten a call like this. No one had.

One of my teachers said, "Buy a whistle. When they call you, blast it into their ears."

"I don't know if they have ears. All I ever get is this hum."

"But try the whistle," said my teacher. "It might work."

But no matter what I tried—whistling, humming back, hanging up—the calls continued as before.

*   *   *

The phone rang.

"Hello?"

Hhmmmmmmm . . .

"Who is this?" I asked. "What do you want?"

Hhhmmmmmmmmmmmm . . .

I waited. The vibration became deeper and deeper.

HHHHMMMMMMMMMMMMMMM . . .

"I'm not hanging up until you tell me who you are."

Suddenly the humming stopped. A living silence gathered itself together. I could feel it coming over the wires, creeping out, surrounding me like a mist.

"Hello? Is anybody there?"

"Wweee're hhhhere," said a muffled voice that sounded not quite human.

"Who is it?" I asked. "Answer me!"

"Us, us, ussssssss . . ."

I cleared my throat. "It's about time you talked! What's the big idea?"

Loud laughter that was both high- and low-pitched came over the receiver. "J-J-J-J-J-Jerrrremmmmy."

"Who are you?" I demanded again.

"Someone you know very well . . ." The voice was echo and squeal, cello and viola, wind and water.

"Elise??? Grover?? Bill??"

"No . . . you're not even warm. Or cold, either. You can do better—better—than that."

28

"Mr. Roman? Debbie next-door? Susie the midget?"

"Terrible guesses, terrible guesses."

I could feel my face getting hot. "Will you quit playing games? I want to know who you are! Right now!"

Suddenly there were two voices.

"What is going on?" I cried. "Tell me now!"

"We're your double." The voices had merged once more. "And the double of your double."

"What are you talking about?"

"We're you. And you're us."

I sighed in exasperation. These guys were nuts. "If you're me," I said, playing along, "why do you call me all the time?"

"To hear the sound of your voice," bellowed one of them.

"We're incomplete without you."

"At sea and lost."

"Pale and incorporeal."

"Do you have bodies? Faces? What do you look like?"

"We look like you, silly."

"We both have curly brown hair."

"And skinny legs."

"Don't forget that scar above the eyebrow."

"And the cut in the lower corner of our right palm."

I turned my hand over and studied it. Sure enough, there was a fresh cut in the lower corner. How had they learned that?

"How do you know that?" I asked.

"We do everything you do," they said.

"We live in your house, wear your clothes, eat your food, and hang out with your friends . . ."

"I've never seen you," I protested.

"We've been invisible—indivisible, hardly existing," they said together. "That's why we keep trying to call you."

"We want to live where we belong. With you."

The voices whispered, one in each ear. They told me what I had done that day and the day before. They described a rock I carried in my pocket for luck, told me how many pieces of gum I chewed each day, and the color of my underwear.

I rubbed my face. Two voices who knew everything about me? Who looked like me down to the last hangnail? Who hung on my every word? Who wanted nothing more than to be with me? What kind of a joke was this?

"Sorry, not buying today," I said, and hung up the phone.

II.

The next morning, when I sat up in bed, they were there. I stretched my arms. *Bam!*

"Ow! Ow! Watch it, will you?" I heard.

"You just poked me in the nose," the other voice said.

"You got me in the chin."

"And you weren't very polite last night."

"Not nice to hang up on your own selves."

"Sorry," I muttered. This was no joke. The phone was one thing, but now they were in my bed! How was I going to get them out of here?

"Where are you?" I asked.

"Right here. Here."

"Where?" I kicked out.

"Watch our toes!"

I swatted the air around me. "Where *are* you?"

"With you. By you. We are you."

I jumped out of bed and looked in the mirror, half thinking I'd see them, or at least a faint double vibration in the air around my head. But all I saw was the bed, bureau, and desk. And my own face and body. No more.

Something flickered at the corner of my eye. Then I saw them. A version of my own face and body—in duplicate—on either side of the bed. They looked quite a bit younger, almost too young for school. Their faces were pudgy and babyish; their legs were kicking restlessly.

They were unmistakably me.

My brother knocked on the door. "Jeremy! Mom says get your head out of the clouds. Breakfast is ready. Hurry up or you'll be late for school."

I went to the closet to get a T-shirt.

"I don't think you should wear that one," said a high voice to my left. "You've already worn it four days this week."

"Wear it," said the other. "It's so good-looking. No one will notice if it smells a little."

I pulled on the T-shirt. It *did* smell. I took it off and sorted through my clothes.

"The blue one," said the deep voice.

I reached for it.

"Yellow," said the high one.

I grabbed another T-shirt from the bottom of the pile. "All right! I'm going to wear this one! Good-bye!"

"We're coming with you."

"No! I don't want you!"

"But we've waited so long to be together," said one of them.

"You're part of us," said the other. "We can't be separated. We're part of you."

"Evermore," they said together. "Evermore."

III.

In homeroom my doubles pinched my fingers during the Pledge of Allegiance.

They made fun of the principal's morning talk.

They sang loudly in my ear during roll call.

I could feel them next to me, one on either side, bumping lightly against my shoulders and legs. They were like two clouds, like two breezy winds. Sometimes they merged and moved around me. And they talked constantly.

I kept tripping over their feet, banging into their elbows. When I thought one was to the left, he was to the right. When I thought the other was in front of me, he was at my side.

They had always been with me—that's what they said—but it had never been like *this* before.

"How come you never bothered me before?" I asked.

"You didn't want to listen," one of them said.

"We were doing things but you couldn't feel them," said the other.

"Now you've talked to us," they both said. "Now you've seen us."

"This means you can annoy me and tease me?" I demanded.

"We're just playing!"

"Don't you have a sense of humor?"

"He must," one of them said. "*We* do."

*   *   *

In gym they whirled around me as if I were a maypole. I stumbled over my own feet, fumbled the ball, and crashed into the other kids on my team. The coach ordered me to sit down until my head cleared.

At lunchtime they argued over what I should eat. I ended up with three salads, two rice puddings, and a plate of grilled cheese sandwiches.

And in math class they whispered answers to my teacher's questions. The wrong answers. So many wrong answers, I couldn't think.

"Sssshhh!" I hissed.

"Don't you like us?" one asked plaintively in his high-pitched voice.

"No!"

"Jeremy . . ." The math teacher was frowning at me.

"Well, you're stuck with us," boomed the other, and planted a loud, smacking kiss on my check. Just like a six-year-old. Come to think of it, that's how old they had looked when I had seen them on either side of the bed. Just what I needed, getting stuck with two imma-ture versions of myself.

One of them tickled me under the chin.

I fell out of my chair, tripped, and crashed to the floor.

"Are you all right?" the teacher asked, standing above me. "You seem nervous today." He helped me to my feet.

"I'm fine," I said. "It's nothing, really."

"Well, really," huffed one of them from behind me. "Nothing? Is that how you talk about yourself?"

"Hardly nothing, dear," said the high-pitched voice. I couldn't tell where *he* was.

I batted the air around me. "Go away."

The teacher stared.

"Not you!" I said. "I was talking to—um—"

"Do you need to go to the nurse's office? You don't seem to be all here today," the teacher said.

"On the contrary," I groaned. "Too much of me is here."

* * *

"That was fun, fun," they said on the way home. "We like going to school with you."

"Where is your home?" I asked. "I'm taking you there."

"Why, we live with you, dear," piped one double, whose shrill voice was beginning to get on my nerves.

"You," echoed the other.

"Where did you live before you met me?"

They giggled. "With you! But you never listened to

us. So we had to phone you."

"You were the one," they said. "The one we were destined for."

"We love you," they said.

I wondered how you got rid of your own selves.

"You can't get rid of us," they said. "We're here to stay."

I didn't even have to say anything. They had heard me thinking. I flung out my arms. "I can't stand it! You never leave me alone!"

"Watch it, will you?" complained one of them.

"So clumsy, isn't he?" said the other.

"You messed up my entire day!" I yelled. "I wish I had hung up on you before you even called!"

"Sorry, so sorry," they said with a little sob. "We'll try not to do it again."

I bounded up the stairs to my house. I wanted to run away, to slam the front door in their faces, to leave them behind forever. They were so annoying. So persistent. So immature. So ignorant.

But they were me. And I was stuck with them.

IV.

They didn't talk for a while after that. I could feel them around me, though, like a patch of cooler air next to my arms and head.

I did my homework. I heard them whispering in the corner of the room. Then they came back to my side.

The air around me rippled, and I could see them. They

looked like they had grown up a bit. Now they looked about eight and a half. One was eating a peanut butter sandwich; the other was pretending to fly a paper airplane.

"We're sorry, Jeremy," whispered the one with the sandwich.

"Really sorry," said the other one, running his hand over his paper airplane.

They spoke in soft, soothing voices.

"We won't do it again."

"No, not ever."

"We want to help you."

"Not hinder you."

"If you want to help me, leave me alone! I mean it!"

They faded away then, with a few stifled sobs. I didn't hear from them again that night, though I could feel their presence everywhere.

*   *   *

I sensed them around me the next morning when I woke up and when I sat down to breakfast. They got on the school bus and followed me to homeroom. But they didn't say a word. At first I enjoyed it.

After a while their silence made me uneasy.

In English class that afternoon they reappeared. I had to write a story. As usual I couldn't think what to put down. I wrote a few boring sentences about my last birthday.

"No, no," said two voices right in my ear. "You're on the wrong track."

"Go away! I'm trying to concentrate."

"Your story is not original. You can do better than that."

"Not if you keep talking at me!" I bent over my paper.

"Don't write that trash. And watch those elbows."

"Can I get back to my story?" I tried to brush them away, but they wouldn't leave.

"Listen!" scolded one of them. "We know what we're talking about."

"I thought you weren't going to bother me anymore."

"We're helping you," said the other. "Trust us."

"We know how to improve your story."

"We'll tell you just what to do."

"All right, all right." They couldn't do much worse than I had done. I crumpled up my paper and took out a fresh sheet.

"My two lost selves showed up yesterday . . . ," one of them whispered in my ear.

I wrote the words down on the paper. They spoke out one line after another. I hoped this didn't count as cheating. They were my own selves, weren't they? After a while it seemed like my own mind talking to me.

I was done before anyone else in the class and handed in my paper. Then I sat down at my desk and watched the teacher read my story.

She read it once, twice. Then she called me over. "Where did you get this idea?"

"From myself," I answered, hoping that was close enough to the truth.

She beamed at me. "That is the true source of inspiration."

I smiled weakly at her. "Actually it was dictated to me

. . . by myselves, I mean."

"You feel you are guided?" Mrs. Adams asked. "Many great artists speak of voices dictating to them . . ."

"We told you, we told you," they gloated.

I pretended not to hear them.

Mrs. Adams looked at my paper again. "This is so different from your usual writing."

"Yeah," I said.

"You seem different today," she continued. "Fuller, richer." She stared at me intently.

"Yes, there is more to you than I thought," she said softly.

The two of them snickered.

"You have unrealized potential," said Mrs. Adams. "A gem in the rough. I didn't know you had it in you."

"We all have parts of ourselves we don't know," I said.

"Wise beyond your years," said Mrs. Adams. "I've just decided to give you an A for this marking period."

The bell rang. I gathered up my books.

"And I look forward to reading more of these wonderful compositions!" Mrs. Adams called after me as I left the classroom.

*   *   *

"That was great," I said in the hallway. "That was amazing."

"Wait," said one. His voice was different, softer, mellower. "More is to come."

The other giggled. His laugh was less high-pitched now.

*   *   *

Every night they showed themselves to me. Each time

they got closer to my age, looked more like me. Their voices were changing, too. More and more they were becoming mirror images of me.

They hadn't been kidding about helping me. It was as if I had the power of three. One day I was fumbling, bumbling, and failing; now I was almost superhuman.

I got a perfect score on an extremely difficult social studies test.

I sang a solo in chorus. Usually my voice cracked and wobbled, but suddenly I had power and range.

During basketball practice, I almost single-handedly won the game for my team.

I wrote another "brilliant" composition for Mrs. Adams.

At home the two of them helped me clean the basement, the attic, and the backyard. My mother was astounded. "You've done the work of three," she said.

"Have I ever," I said.

"You need us, you need us," they chanted in my ear. "You need us as much as we need you."

I was starting to think they were right.

*   *   *

It went on like that for three weeks. I was the first kid chosen for any team. The teachers praised me to the skies. My mother doubled my allowance. Everyone loved me.

When I thanked my doubles they said, "Helping you is helping ourselves."

"We're planning for the future," they said.

I thought of my own future—of all the A's on my report cards, the parties thrown just for me, the rewards from my parents. "Sounds good," I said. "Keep on planning."

I heard them turning the pages of my math book. I didn't even have to study anymore.

V.

One night I was reading in bed. My doubles had been quiet for a while—they were dozing, I thought, or planning the events of the next day.

"Good night, everybody." I leaned over to turn off the light.

Suddenly they appeared next to me in the bed. They were wearing pajamas just like mine. They were smiling. Their fingers had jam stains on them in exactly the same spots as mine.

"Hey, what's up?" I asked.

"Move over," said the self on my left.

"Scoot," said the one on the right.

"Move over yourself. This is *my* bed."

"It's our bed," they said together.

I laughed loudly.

"You have to leave," said the one on the left.

"Right now."

"What kind of a joke is this?" I asked.

"No joke."

"Why should we joke? We're very serious."

They reached across me as if I weren't even there and

began to whisper to each other.

"This is my bed. Get out!" I cried.

"Who's talking?" one of them asked.

"I don't hear anyone talking."

"Don't see anyone, either."

"No one here but us."

I stood up on the bed. "Cut it out! Now!"

They rolled toward the center of the bed, shoving against me.

I tried to push them back, but my legs and arms suddenly had no strength.

One of them lifted his finger and flicked me off the bed. I flew to the other side of the room and landed in the corner where they used to spend the nights. My body felt light, weightless, empty.

"What's happening!?" I was breathless. I couldn't feel my fingers and toes.

"Do you hear something?" asked one. He was leaning toward the other, smiling.

"Not me. Just another boring quiet school night."

I couldn't seem to control my body anymore. "Hey!" I yelled.

"It's nice, just the two of us here," said one of them, licking a spot of jam off his finger.

"I'm here!" I cried. "Can't you see me?"

"It's good to have peace and quiet for a change."

"No disturbances."

"No annoying noises in the background."

"I'm not a noise! I belong here! This is *my* room!"

41

They looked at each other, sighed, and closed their eyes.

"Good night," they said to each other. "Good night."

"I'm Jeremy!" I called. "Jeremy, Jeremy, Jeremy!"

No one answered me.

I rushed to the mirror. But it only reflected two boys wearing pajamas, with jam on their fingers, who lay with eyes closed on either side of my bed.

"What about me? Where am I?"

The surface of the mirror rippled as if my image were hiding somewhere deep inside.

*　　*　　*

There was a knock on the door, and my mother came into the room.

"Mom!" I cried. "Mom! Help! What's happening to me?"

"Good night, twins!" my mother said. "Shut off that light! We don't want you tired for school again, do we?"

"No, Mother," said one of them.

"We'll go right to sleep," said the other.

"Mom . . . ," I cried in a voice that sounded high and tinny.

"Sweet dreams, Jerry," said my mother. "And you, too, Marty." She bent over the bed and kissed them good night. Then she turned off the light and tiptoed out of the room.

VI.

I call them every day now. When they pick up the phone, there's a humming sound, a low vibration on the other end. Usually they hang up right away. But they're beginning to forget me—who I am and what I want.

The day will come when they will wonder: Who is trying to reach us? Then they will stay on the phone and listen. They will be frightened, then intrigued. My voice—rusty and trembling—will come over the lines. Once I have spoken the first words, I will start to take back my life.

7

STUCK

I'm stuck between two worlds. You might think this is rather a tight place to be, but actually I have room to maneuver. And on certain days I can see both worlds quite clearly, though never at the same time.

Where I am—it seems to be some kind of resting place—is a small room. The walls are a yellowish color. There is a stove where I can cook and a bed that I lie down on when I'm tired.

There are two windows on opposite sides of the room. Through one I see a grassy meadow; through the other, city streets thronged with people.

There is no one in this room but me.

*   *   *

In the morning I get up and make my bed. I take milk and eggs out of the refrigerator and cook a little breakfast. There is always food in the refrigerator—not much, it's true, and always the same—but I'm never very hungry.

When breakfast is done, I do my exercises. I clean the room—though it never seems to get dirty—and it's time for lunch. A sandwich, a glass of juice, a biscuit. Then I nap.

When I wake up, I go to one window and then I go to the other one. Depending on what I see, I may spend hours or minutes at each one. Sometimes I run from one window to the other, back and forth, almost madly. Exhausted, I lie down until supper and think about what I have seen.

*   *   *

How long have I been here? Forever, I think. I don't remember anything that came before. Occasionally I get out. Not all of me, of course. Sometimes I press my hand against the window and feel it giving way, slowly dissolving under my touch. With a little more pressure I can wiggle a finger free, or even shove an elbow or a foot into one world or another for a few minutes.

Once I put my hand through the green window and felt the sun warming my skin. A breeze came into my room, and I heard birds chirping and the sound of lawn mowers cutting grass.

For the rest of the day I felt the sunlight, as though a bright room had opened up inside me.

Another time I thrust my head out the city window. The air was a sooty gray. Pigeons circled a marble building with busts of men and women on it. People rushed past me. I tried to talk to them, but they didn't hear me. One person saw me—an old woman with a chalk-white face who was brushing her teeth over the gutter. She muttered something to herself and then turned away.

*   *   *

Years ago the room was different. It was plainer. The bed was a mattress on the floor. The table was smaller. There were no windows in the walls.

One day I began to scratch and scrape at the walls. At first I used my fingernails, then a piece of wood, then a knife. Paint chips fell to the floor as I scraped off layer after layer of paint. The chips clung to my skin, embedded themselves in my scalp, worked their way under my fingernails. They collected in piles around my feet. Yet, no matter how much I scraped, there was always another layer to uncover.

I remember the morning I first saw the windows. For a long time I stood between them, looking from one to the other, half expecting them to dissolve, evaporate, disappear as mysteriously as they had appeared. I walked toward them with slow, hesitant steps. I didn't know where to go first.

But finally I touched one. I remember how it felt—a smooth, cool surface, like water, only firmer to the touch. And then I looked. I saw movement, color, and light. The forms were indistinct, but as I stared at them they slowly became clearer. Day after day I spent more and more hours with my face pressed against one window or the other—until, one day, I don't know why, I pressed my hand firmly against the window and it gave way. Just a few inches, enough to push my fingers through. Then I breathed the air of a new world.

*   *   *

I haven't been able to get out for a while—not so much as a fingertip through a window—and I'm beginning to wonder if this room is the only world. Perhaps those other two are mirages or even pictures painted cleverly on the walls. Have I hallucinated the sunlight and the old woman?

In which case, I am not stuck between two worlds—but trapped in this one.

No, it can't be. My hand went through and, once, my head. It happened; I know it happened.

I won't accept that the boundaries of my world are four yellowish walls.

I have a plan. I am going to escape. I will hurl myself through a window. Which one, I haven't decided yet. Really it doesn't matter. Then, instead of a plain room with a stove and a bed, I will be sitting in an empty meadow or rushing along city streets.

Then I will be free.

Free of my room forever.

Only one thing worries me. When I'm outside at last, I wonder if I will find myself trapped once more, caught—and longing to get back to my room.

8

THIN

The boy's name was Thin. He was small and bony, with a narrow nose and mouth and large, luminous eyes that he kept half shut, as though he did not want anyone to see the expression behind his lids. He was good at dodging complaints, demands, and blows. He knew how to disappear, too. And then reappear when there was food around.

It was well known that Thin would do anything for food.

*　　*　　*

At lunchtime the children filed into the cafeteria, stood in line, piled their lunch trays with food. Then they sat down at long gray tables with their trays in front of them. What did they have to eat? A greasy slice of roast beef. Some limp peas. A puddle of applesauce and a dry cake with cinnamon and nuts.

And there was Thin. No one ever saw him with a tray. He didn't have money to buy lunch. Perhaps he brought his lunch from home; perhaps he didn't. Perhaps he ate it on the way to school; perhaps someone took it from him. No matter. He was always hungry.

He went from table to table, wheedling, pleading, begging.

The children tossed him cakes and watched him jump for them. They rolled peas to him one by one. They slid pieces of roast beef over the edge of the table and watched him scramble to catch them as they fell to the dirty brown linoleum floor.

He had been known to eat food off the floor.

He dusted it off, stuffed it into his mouth, and went on to the next table.

He was always hungry.

*   *   *

One day, as a game, all the children in the cafeteria handed him their dishes of ice cream. He started near the window and worked his way through the room, gobbling down one dessert after another. The children stamped their feet and clapped their hands as he swallowed dozens of bowls of ice cream. He didn't even bother to pick up a spoon, just dumped the entire contents of the dishes into his mouth.

But the next day he was hungry again.

*   *   *

49

Thin would beg, stand on his head, play, steal, fight, or cry for a sweet.

He grabbed at a licorice stick that a boy held out to him. The boy raised his hand as if to strike him. Thin cringed. The boy laughed and tossed the licorice stick at him.

Thin devoured it.

"Come to my house tonight," the boy said, staring at him with dull black eyes.

Thin watched him warily.

"I have candy; lots of candy."

After school Thin followed him home.

The black-eyed boy gave him candy and more candy. Marzipan people, chocolate deer and fish and dogs, yellow marshmallow puffs, white sugar chicks, pieces of nut-filled fudge . . .

Thin ate it all, grabbing it up with quick, slender fingers.

"There's more candy in the shed," said the black-eyed boy.

As soon as Thin was inside, the boy slammed the door and locked him in.

The shed was damp and smelled like rotting boards. Thin pushed against the door, but it didn't yield. Through a window streaked with dust, he saw the other boy's round face watching him.

"More candy?" the boy taunted. "Want more candy?"

*   *   *

The next morning, the boy came and opened the door.

Thin picked himself up and ran toward the street on his spindly legs. Behind him the boy called out. "I have candy! Candy!"

Thin stopped. He lowered his eyes. Beneath half-closed lids, his luminous eyes gleamed.

The boy walked over to Thin. He reached into his pocket and took out a piece of half-eaten chocolate wrapped in crumpled foil. Thin snatched it from the boy's hand, tore off the wrapping, and stuffed the chocolate into his mouth.

With a smile the boy pulled out a white marshmallow rabbit whose head had been torn off.

Thin ate that, too.

The boy gave him a slice of jellied candy with a few specks of dirt clinging to it. Thin didn't notice. He ate a chewed licorice stick, a soggy piece of cookie, and a handful of discolored jelly beans. Then he held out his hands for more.

"That's it," the boy said, rubbing the side of his face with dirty fingers. He gave Thin a push but Thin did not move. Instead, he shoved his bony fingers into the boy's shirt pocket and brought out a lint-covered gum-drop.

"I don't have any more," the boy said. "You got all my candy now."

Thin thrust his hands into the boy's other pockets. A few small candies tumbled into his hand. He swallowed them instantly, then searched the boy's pockets again. There was nothing in them. Thin poked them, slapped them, turned them inside out. The candy was all gone.

Thin seized the boy's shoulders.

"Stop!" the boy cried as Thin shook him, tore off his shirt, and pummeled his back and arms. But Thin did not listen. He pounded the boy's flesh as if it would yield up secret caches of candy, as if the boy were a tree of delights that needed only to be shaken to rain its treasures on the ground.

The boy screamed as if he were being devoured.

9

THE PERFECT BED

Once, long ago, there was a young girl who could not sleep on any bed.

She left her home and went from house to house, searching for the perfect bed, but she could never find one.

First she tried her friends.

They offered her their thickest mattresses, their softest pillows, their downiest quilts.

"The best," they said.

"I hope so," she said, turning off the light and pulling the covers over herself.

They tiptoed out of the room.

"How was it?" they asked eagerly the next morning.

"The sheets scratched my skin so!" She held up her arms, which were red and irritated. "And there was a lump on the side of the mattress. I couldn't sleep a wink!"

The friends sighed.

Then they saw her pale, exhausted face, the dark circles under her eyes, her limping gait as she crossed the kitchen to pour herself a cup of tea.

"We're sorry," they said.

"I don't know how I am going to make it through the day," she moaned. "And I have to find a resting place tonight."

"Have you tried the neighbors?" they asked. "The people across the street? They travel all the time, have the best taste. Everyone knows they have the smoothest sheets and the most expensive mattresses, imported from the other side of the world."

That night she knocked on the neighbors' door, and they led her to a beautiful room decorated with tapestries on the wall and glowing carpets on the floor. The bed was luxurious, covered with the finest sheets and the thickest blankets. Still she couldn't sleep. The silk sheets had tiny creases on the edges. There was a speck of dust on the pillow that made her sneeze all night.

She lay in the bed and thought.

*   *   *

Once, long ago, she had slept soundly every night in the same bed. Her mattress was lumpy, her sheets were coarsely woven, and her pillow was flat in places. But she was happy. When the window was open, a breeze woke her in the morning. Sunlight fell across her face. She used to leap out of bed and run down the stairs.

No one worried about her. And she was never tired.

Then her best friend came to stay.

"I'll sleep on the floor," she said to her friend. "It won't matter to me."

The friend took the bed. In the morning the girl asked her friend how she had slept.

"Oh, terribly!" said the friend. "Your sheets were so rough, they made my skin itch all night. And how do you sleep on that flat pillow? It was just like putting my head on a board!"

The girl was astonished. "I thought you would be comfortable there," she said. "I am."

Her best friend laughed, not kindly. "You don't know any better, do you? Insensitivity is bliss!"

The girl reached over and touched the sheets. For the first time she felt the bumps of the threads, the knotted seams, the uneven grain of the cloth. The coarse material abraded her fingertips and sent a strange sensation into her hands and arms. It was as though she were being awakened.

*   *   *

When she had exhausted the list of friends—and friends of friends—she began to knock on strangers' doors.

"Do you have a comfortable bed for the night?" she asked. She was bone tired, drenched, her hair dripping icy water down her face and back.

The strangers took her in. They gave her warm, dry clothing to put on. They fed her supper, then led her to the room with their softest bed.

"We hope you sleep well," they said.

She could barely nod, she was so tired.

But in the morning it was always the same story. The pillow had a loose thread that tickled her all night. The mattress label had bruised her skin. A clump of feathers in the comforter had bumped her leg.

She tried all the beds. And found them all wanting.

*   *   *

All those days in the rain and the sun, searching for the perfect night's rest!

And all the time getting less and less sleep.

Her friends worried about her. Her health couldn't hold up much longer. And what kind of a life was it, wandering from door to door, asking strangers for a bed for the night?

They tried to reason with her. She was too sensitive, too demanding, they said. This world wasn't perfect. She had to recognize that and accept it. Make her adjustments. Change her attitude. Sleep with a loose thread or little lump here or there.

She wouldn't listen. She couldn't. She was aching, bruised, weary. All she could think about was a good night's sleep.

And then it happened. She found the perfect bed.

In a small house at the edge of the woods, a woman answered her knock.

"We heard you were coming." She showed her into the house.

The woman helped the girl off with her coat and boots. She rubbed her hair dry with a towel, brought her a hot drink and a clean nightgown of the finest cloth.

And while the girl sat and sipped her drink, the woman spoke to her in low soothing tones. "We have prepared the very best bed for you. It took us three months to make it. No one in the world can equal this bed. You will have a long, profound, and restful sleep."

The girl stared at her in disbelief.

The woman took the girl by the hand and led her into a room where thick mattresses were piled high, almost to the ceiling, and each one was covered with a silk sheet.

"One hundred mattresses," the woman announced proudly. "Filled with goose down, especially ordered from every corner of the world. Handwoven covers and hand-stitched seams. And it is for you. All you have to do is lie down and sleep."

The words alone were almost enough to put the girl to sleep. She could feel herself sinking down as she listened—down into a dark, warm place where she didn't have to think or understand, where nothing was asked of her except to breathe.

The woman brought a ladder and steadied it as the girl sleepily climbed to the top and lay down on the bed. The pillow was soft as a breath of air and the blanket was like a wing. The air was scented as if from masses of invisible flowers. There were no bumps anywhere, only an enveloping warmth. The bed seemed to curl itself and nestle around her, as though it were a living being that existed only for her comfort.

"Come sleep, come sleep," the bed seemed to say. "The perfect bed for the perfect person."

She sighed once, closed her eyes, and almost against her will, fell into a deep, dreamless sleep.

*   *   *

She awoke late at night. What or who had awoken her? Her throat was dry, she could scarcely breathe. The room was dark; she could see nothing. The scent of flowers was gone. The air was dry, suffocating, and flat. But the bed still curled around her like a living thing.

She tried to get up. The bed pulled her down. Its comfort was devastating.

Her tongue was like a stone in her mouth. Her arms and legs lay uselessly at her side. Time was infinite. Nothing happened and nothing ever would. How long had she been asleep? Minutes, hours, days, weeks? Or perhaps years, centuries, ages?

As she lay in the darkness, all of her previous wanderings seemed like a haven, a paradise of movement and freedom. She thought back to the people she had met, the beds she had tried to sleep in, the places she had traveled. Had she now lost it all?

*   *   *

Some time later, with infinite patience and will, she slowly moved a finger. Then she sank back, exhausted, onto the nest of pillows.

As she lay there catching her breath, she noticed that the pillow was not quite as comfortable as it had been a moment before.

Slowly, tentatively, she turned her head an inch to the left. The sheets suddenly felt clammy.

Her hands trembled. A small feather worked its way loose from the comforter, and its quill scratched her skin.

A shout of joy tore from her throat. She sat up, threw off the bedding, scrambled down the ladder, and ran from the house.

*　　*　　*

Many years, many beds later, she sat in a garden with a friend. She never stayed in one place for long. People were always ready to welcome her, invite her in. She slept well now—at least some of the time.

A friend asked her what she had learned from her years of wandering from house to house.

"When you find the perfect bed, run from it," she said. "If you lie down in that bed, you will never get up."

10

THROUGH THE MIRROR

What would you do if your world disappeared? If it hung shining like a bit of water suspended from a leaf, and then the wind blew and shattered it on the ground? If the walls of your room suddenly dissolved and you were standing in a forest, a dark forest with waving ferns. What would you do then?

Actually, it didn't happen just like that. It happened like this. Sandra was sitting in her bedroom, staring into the mirror. She was a pretty girl with flushed cheeks and curly, fine hair, with a green ribbon pinned on the side. A girl with the satisfied look of one pampered by her family, petted by her teachers, and doted on by her friends. A girl accustomed to winning, to getting what she wanted. To always having the best of everything.

But now Sandra's face had an expression of shock and disbelief. Because the face that stared back from the mirror was different from hers. The hair was thick and tangled. The face was dirty.

"And I just washed," Sandra muttered to herself. She wondered if the mirror was dirty. She rubbed it a bit, and the girl on the other side put up an arm as if to protect herself.

Sandra stopped and stared. The dirty girl dropped her arm and grinned. Sandra recoiled a little but then leaned forward. "Who are you?" she asked. "What are you doing here?"

"What are you doing here?" the dirty girl mimicked.

Sandra held up her hand as if to push the other girl deeper into the mirror.

The dirty girl pushed back.

"Go away!" Sandra said. "Leave me alone!"

The other girl reached forward and yanked her into the mirror.

Sandra saw a flash of pink that could have been her bedspread. She saw the girl with the tangled, dirty hair leap through a door that seemed to melt into the air. And then her room was gone. She was in a forest. A dark forest with curling ferns tipped with light.

She found herself on a path full of pine needles and pinecones, thorny branches, shriveled apples, and tiny blackened stones. The sky was very high above, bits of blue falling through the overhanging trees like scraps of ragged cloth. In the shadowy forest a harsh voice called her name. Sandra sat down, put her face in her hands, and cried.

Meanwhile, in a small white house, a girl with tangled hair was washing her face. She picked up a brush and pulled it through her hair. She fastened a ribbon—a red ribbon—in her curls.

When she looked in the mirror, she smiled. The mirror image smiled back. The red ribbon bobbed in her curly, fine hair. Her cheeks were flushed and her eyes sparkled. She leaned over, tied her sneakers, and skipped down the stairs.

11

SWAN SISTER

Each night my seven brothers change into swans and fly out the doors, the windows, the chimney. The air is thick with feathers and dust. After my brothers have flown over the yard and out of sight, I, their younger sister, creep out of the house to pick up the feathers that lie on the dark grass like glowing swords.

The house is silent after they have left, and I go up to my room, where I pull the covers tightly around me. I lie awake, straining to hear the long, high calls that come through the window more and more faintly. When at last they cease, I fall asleep, though my nights are restless and troubled by dreams.

*　　*　　*

As a small child I stood on a dark lawn as seven white swans alighted in a circle around me. I held out pieces of crumbled bread, which they plucked delicately from my infant hand. It was just before dawn, and I had come out of bed early to see them. Then the swans rose in the air and disappeared into a small woods nearby. "Swans, come back!" I cried. "Swans, come back!"

Soon my seven brothers came out of the woods. They picked me up on their shoulders and threw me into the air, pretending to make me fly.

"Swans!" I sobbed.

My brothers bounced balls, gave me candy, showed me books. But I refused to be consoled, and cried straight through to the night—when seven swans appeared in our living room and beat at the doors and windows until I let them out.

*   *   *

When I was a little older and understood that my brothers were the swans and the swans my brothers, I wanted to join them.

One evening when they came home from work, I ladled out the soup and heated the coffee. My brothers sat slumped at the table, not saying much, only glancing anxiously at the sky. Sometimes they dozed between spoonfuls of soup, and then I tapped them on the shoulders until they jerked awake.

When they were done eating they rose and went to the living room. I followed, asking questions. "Do you sleep in the air?"

My eldest brother looked out the window, and his eyes seemed to brighten. "Never."

"Are you scared of falling?" I asked my second brother.

Sometimes as I lay in bed at night, I imagined them falling to earth—the great wings collapsing, bright eyes closing—and animals of the forest finding them and tearing their flesh. I saw them caught in trees, hung on wires. Then I woke with a gasp and a cry and could not sleep again for hours.

My brother laughed. "Why scared? Swans don't fall. And even if I falter, the others will catch me. But it has never happened."

"What is it like?" I asked.

My brothers gazed out the windows, checked their watches, stroked their arms impatiently.

"What is what like?" my second brother said.

"The change . . . you know."

He whirled around, turned his back to me, as if protecting something I could not see.

My other brothers smiled at me and shook their heads. My eldest brother patted me on the back.

"Won't you tell me what it's like?" I pleaded.

The sun plummeted suddenly downward. It grew dark. My brothers stood motionless, scarcely breathing. Then their sturdy limbs, their strong legs and arms, dwindled into nothing and reformed—from a breath of air—into large wings, sharp beaks, and downy feathers. It seemed then that they wanted to speak to me, to answer my questions, but only strange, high-pitched cries issued from their throats as they burst free, flying through the doors and windows into the night sky.

*   *   *

I began to practice jumping, at first from our porch, then from the low branches of a tree. I spread out my arms, closed my eyes tightly, and imagined myself soaring. Yet, time after time, I fell straight to the ground, twisting ankles and bruising my legs.

My brothers looked at me, worried.

"Where did you get those bruises?"

"I fell. It was nothing."

"From where?"

"Out of the tree."

"The tree! What were you doing there?"

"Trying to fly."

My brothers frowned. "You'll only hurt yourself that way."

"Then show me how."

My eldest brother stroked his arms as if they were covered with invisible feathers. "We can't."

"Why not?"

They exchanged glances.

"Why won't you tell me!" I cried. "Why do you keep secrets from me?"

"It's not that," my seventh brother said. He touched my shoulder.

"We'd like to help you," said my second brother. "But we just don't know how."

"You have to find the way for yourself," my oldest brother said. "We did . . ."

*   *   *

I searched their rooms for answers to my questions. I

opened drawers, looked under piles of neatly folded socks, checked beds and mattresses. I felt along windows, lifted rugs, tapped the spines of old schoolbooks. I never found a trace of what I hoped for: a recipe, a message, a clue—even a single word written on a slip of paper, a word that would give me wings.

*   *   *

Then I began to go to the woods behind our house. I gathered leaves, roots, and twigs and crushed them between stones, mixed them with oil, and spread the often foul-smelling mess over my arms, legs, and face. In the morning I examined myself, hoping to see the first downy feathers or perhaps the beginning of a beak.

I bathed in ice-cold water, drank cups of vile-tasting tea.

I arranged swan feathers in intricate patterns and mumbled words over them during different phases of the moon.

Still, each night my brothers left me. They changed into swans. Their wings beat wildly against the walls. The house could not contain their fury and desire. I, too, reached out my arms—held them wide—as if I might also fly. My arms ached and strained, stretched almost out of their sockets.

"Take me with you!" I cried. "I can fly. I can!"

The swan cries of my brothers grew more and more urgent. Their beaks slashed against windows and curtains; their wings dashed against walls, overturning lamps, knocking down pictures.

My arms fell to my sides. I ran to the windows, flung

open the doors. And my brothers flew out in a rush, leaving feathers scattered thick on the rug.

* * *

In the morning my brothers came home. They were muddy, tired, trampled. I gave them cups of coffee and pancakes, eggs, and more coffee. I unlaced their boots, brought them soap and water, helped them into clean clothes. Then, weary-eyed and exhausted, they went off to work.

I cleaned the kitchen, washed the floor. I scrubbed their muddy clothes and put the soup on to simmer until dinner. Then I went to the oak chair in the living room.

My pile of books was waiting. I had discovered them in the attic one night when I couldn't sleep. Old volumes with stiff spines and thick, faded pages that told of men turning into snakes, bears changing into men, birds that flew over prison walls and became young girls, and girls who became birds, who soared in the sky . . .

The lightness, the flight, the swiftness. The wings, the bills, the small eyes, the haunting cries. The wind and the water. The new dangers. How many times I imagined it all, sitting in my rocking chair. I read and read, often not stopping to eat, until the light dimmed and I heard my brothers' steps on the porch.

* * *

Tending daily to my brothers, watching them come in as men and go out as swans, like wheels that turn ceaselessly, I wonder: What is it like to be broken and remade over and over again? And at the moment when they are neither man nor swan, who or what are they?

It seems to me that they are only a breath, only a thought, so fine they could pass through the eye of a needle.

Can I, too, become so fine and smooth, like a piece of silk or a breath of air, that I can turn myself inside out?

* * *

One night as they flew out the windows and doors, I felt the breeze from their wings on my face. I heard their cries growing fainter and fainter. And I pictured myself going with them.

I arched my long, narrow throat forward; I stretched my arms wide and I soared over lakes and forests until I found my brothers. When I was tired, I alighted on a rock and my brothers made a circle around me. Then, when we were rested, we rose into the air.

We were like a white necklace flung into the sky. We were like an arrow shot from a bow. We were bound into swans' bodies, but we were free.

* * *

I have put away my books, potions, and spells. I am through with frantic searches and impatient questions.

When my brothers change into swans each night, I don't chase after them. I sit quietly in a chair. I close my eyes. I watch the flow of my breath as it travels down my spine and through my arms and legs.

Every night I picture myself with my brothers. Each time I make the journey, I feel closer to them.

It has begun to happen. Already I have felt myself dwindle down to nothing, to darkness, to silence. Once a wing erupted from my arm and a wild cry came out of my throat. Once my body became so light it lifted from the chair. Something is stirring, awakening. A great wing is beating through my days.